Sue and Ned's
Treasure Hunt

Written and illustrated
by
S.S. Hall

May Sue and and Ned always bring glory to God.

For my loving husband Gayland, thank you.

Special ❤s and Xs for Dedra Carter,
friend and lover of story

ISBN: 978-0-578-37998-2

Printed in the United States of America
Cover design by S.S. Hall

Hey Ned, we have another question on your *Ask Ned* website. Sydney from Texas asked, "What is the best, most excellent treasure in the whole wide world?"

Wow, that's a big question, Ned. What is the best, most excellent treasure in the whole wide world?

How about we go on a treasure hunt to investigate?

The world is full of all kinds of treasures, and every treasure hunter needs a map. X marks the spot!

Hmm, you know what Ned? It might be hard to choose just one.

Sundaes
$1.50

Scooter's

I was thinking... *maybe* we're not even searching for a thing at all.

Remember when we sent all of those cards to our friends? Everyone was so happy!
That made us happy, too. That was an excellent treasure!

Or maybe...

What about going to Granny's house? Granny is always a hoot, and her milk and cookies are scrumptious. She gives the best bear hugs, too.

A trip to Granny's might be the most excellent treasure!

Or maybe...

Splish Splash!

When God waters the grass and the trees, our feet get to
splish splash in the rain puddles...

...and mom *loves* the mud pies we make for her.

A treasure for sure!

Or maybe...

Sharing ICE CREAM!

I love sharing a sundae with my best friend. Ned, I think God invented ice cream just for friends to share.

What an excellent treasure!

Or maybe...

Wait! What about the beach?

We love the beach!

Isn't sand squishing under your hooves just the best? My toes get happy when they get to wiggle in cool, wet sand.

Building sand castles and jumping in the waves are definitely excellent treasures!

Or maybe...

Snorkeling is like swimming
around in God's crayon box!

I wish my box had all those colors! Do you think swimming with God's sea creatures is the most excellent treasure?

Or maybe...

Oh, wait! What about investigating all the really cool creepy crawlies God has created?
I don't know how He even thought of all of them!

Counting fuzzy legs is a super awesome treasure!

Or maybe...

We can't forget camping in the woods. Roasting marshmallows, hotdogs, and corn ears over a campfire is the best!

When we're in the woods, it's like God gives us our own special playground with trees to climb, funny little animals and colorful birds to watch, and fishing holes full of frogs to catch.

Yes, camping in the woods could be the most excellent treasure.

Or maybe...

Oh, what about the seasons? God made such special times of year for us. Remember how we get to pick a pumpkin from the pumpkin patch each Fall?

God paints the leaves with oranges and yellows and browns. We get to jump into big piles of them!

The seasons are like four treasures wrapped up in one super duper package.

Or maybe...

Ned, we may have found it!

Sunsets are incredible. See how the
oranges and pinks swirl together? I don't
know how God makes his colors do that,
but it sure is pretty.

Maybe sunrises and sunsets are the most excellent treasures.

But then there's an entire universe out there. The stars are beautiful at night. God must have had a whole bag of stardust when he created the heavens.

You know what, Ned? Finding *THE* most excellent treasure in the whole world is harder than I thought it would be.

Ned, of course! Your favorite holiday must be a treasure! I know how you love to wear your Christmas sweater and nibble popcorn from the Christmas tree while I sing Jingle Bells.

Super fun!

Or maybe...

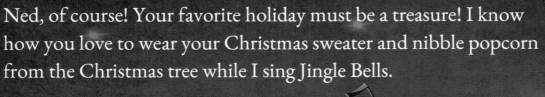

Wait, How could I forget dashing through the snow behind Papaw's big red mule? Doc is super fast! Remember how the snowflakes melted on our tongues? It's magical when God makes it snow!

Sleigh rides might be the most excellent treasure.

Or maybe...

FOR UNTO US A CHILD IS BORN.

YES!

For where your treasure is, there your heart will be also

From the Author

Matthew 6:19-21 NKJV

"Do not lay up for yourselves treasures on earth, where moth and rust destroy and where thieves break in and steal; but lay up for yourselves treasures in heaven, where neither moth nor rust destroys and where thieves do not break in and steal. For where your treasure is, there your heart will be also."

Colossians 2:2-3 NLT

I want them to be encouraged and knit together by strong ties of love. I want them to have complete confidence that they understand God's mysterious plan, which is Christ Himself. In Him lie hidden all the treasures of wisdom and knowledge.

Dear Parents,

God has blessed us with so many treasures in our lives. What treasures are special to your family? Help your child make a treasure map!

SUE'S DIY MAP MAKING

1. Take a sheet of printer paper and crumple it.
2. Uncrumple and place on a cookie sheet or flat dish.
3. Mix a small amount of boiling water and instant coffee.
4. Pour the mixture onto the paper and spread over surface.
5. Let stand for 5 minutes. Blot excess off with paper towels.
6. Bake in preheated oven at 200 degrees for 5 minutes or so until paper is dry.
7. Have fun creating your map of treasures!

Want to know more about Sue and Ned
and how their story came to be?

Visit www.sherryscabin.com/illustrations